SUNBURST CITY
DRAGONS

In loving memory of Cheryl, Grandma Owl.
An incredible lady with a thirst for knowledge,
amazing sense of adventure with unlimited warmth and kindness.
A role model, because how could you not be?

ISBN number: ISBN 978-1-8383080-7-0

First edition August 2021
Author: Jane Huddleston
Illustrations and formatting:
David Robinson

www.sunburstcitydragons.co.uk

MILLIE'S BOOK

Written by
Jane Huddleston

Illustrated by
David Robinson

Outside Sunburst City, where the hills are wild and green,
Live a group of ten old dragons that most humans haven't seen.
They work and have adventures in a secret world of wonder,
While living in a hidden cave that's halfway up Mount Thunder.
They sneak around so humans don't know where they all have been,
Just two brave children help their dragon friends remain unseen.

Theo's a mechanic
Bob announces for the trains
Lucy is an athlete
Harry unblocks drains
Millie is a writer
Olive farms the land
Alice is a scientist
Jack makes chairs by hand
Yellowbeard's a pirate, now retired with creaking knees
Isla is a beekeeper, she's busy keeping bees

HARRY

MILLIE

OLIVE

JACK

YELLOWBEARD

ISLA

Millie is a writer and her scales are navy blue,
She sets her stories anywhere from here to Timbuktu.
She hasn't always written, no, she used to be a cook,
But on her last big birthday thought 'I want to write a book!'

She's eighty eight years old, has been an author now for years,
Her stories make you laugh or leave you crying floods of tears.
She's written lots of books so far, has really been prolific.
Book clubs round the world agree her stories are terrific!

She wants to write a mystery next but lacks the inspiration.
Where to set the story? Pirate ship or railway station?!
She poured a cup of tea, looked to the sky to find ideas.
She'd never been this stuck before through all her writing years.

The page stayed blank, she looked around, saw friends in nearby fields,
Yellowbeard was polishing his stash of golden shields.
With head stuck out her tractor roof, Olive farmed the land,
Harry swept up in the yard, the children lent a hand.

The Sunburst City dragons had two friends who were so helpful,
And in keeping dragons secret they had proven fundamental.
Matt and Alex Walker lived nearby and could be trusted,
They would often help hide dragon clues so none of them got busted.

She thought about the children's help and how they were so great,
At meeting them in secret by their wooden garden gate.
Millie thought of Harry's stories from his holiday,
An island full of secret dragon clans back in the day.

She looked out to the sea as an idea started whirring,
She froze to not disturb the busy brain cells that were stirring.
Theo clanged from far away, fixing bits of wagons,
'That's it!' she thought 'The story's set within a land of dragons!'

She wondered to a meadow thinking what's the mystery,
Perhaps ten humans live in secret, dragons couldn't see.
The special sunny day when this adventure will take place,
Will see an island wide, exciting, speedy dragon race.

How would dragons race on land, it had to be so fast,
Then on the nearby cycle path her friend Bob hurtled past.
'That's it!' Millie exclaimed, 'A race with dragons on their bikes,
A speedy race in sunshine is what everybody likes!'

She grabbed her pen and paper now with inspiration flowing,
She ran into her office so her writing could get going.
The setting was the Isle of Dragons many moons ago,
A shipwreck meant ten humans landed, dragons didn't know.

They built a house and farmed the land whilst keeping very quiet,
They didn't fancy dragons adding humans to their diet.
One sunny day competitors were ready for the race,
From round the world the dragons came to try and win first place.

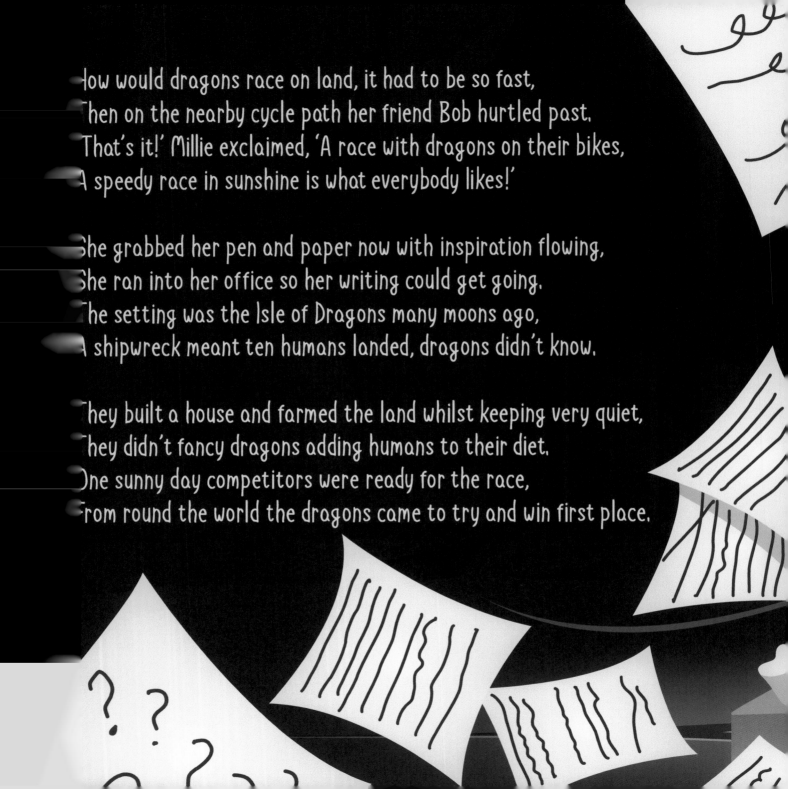

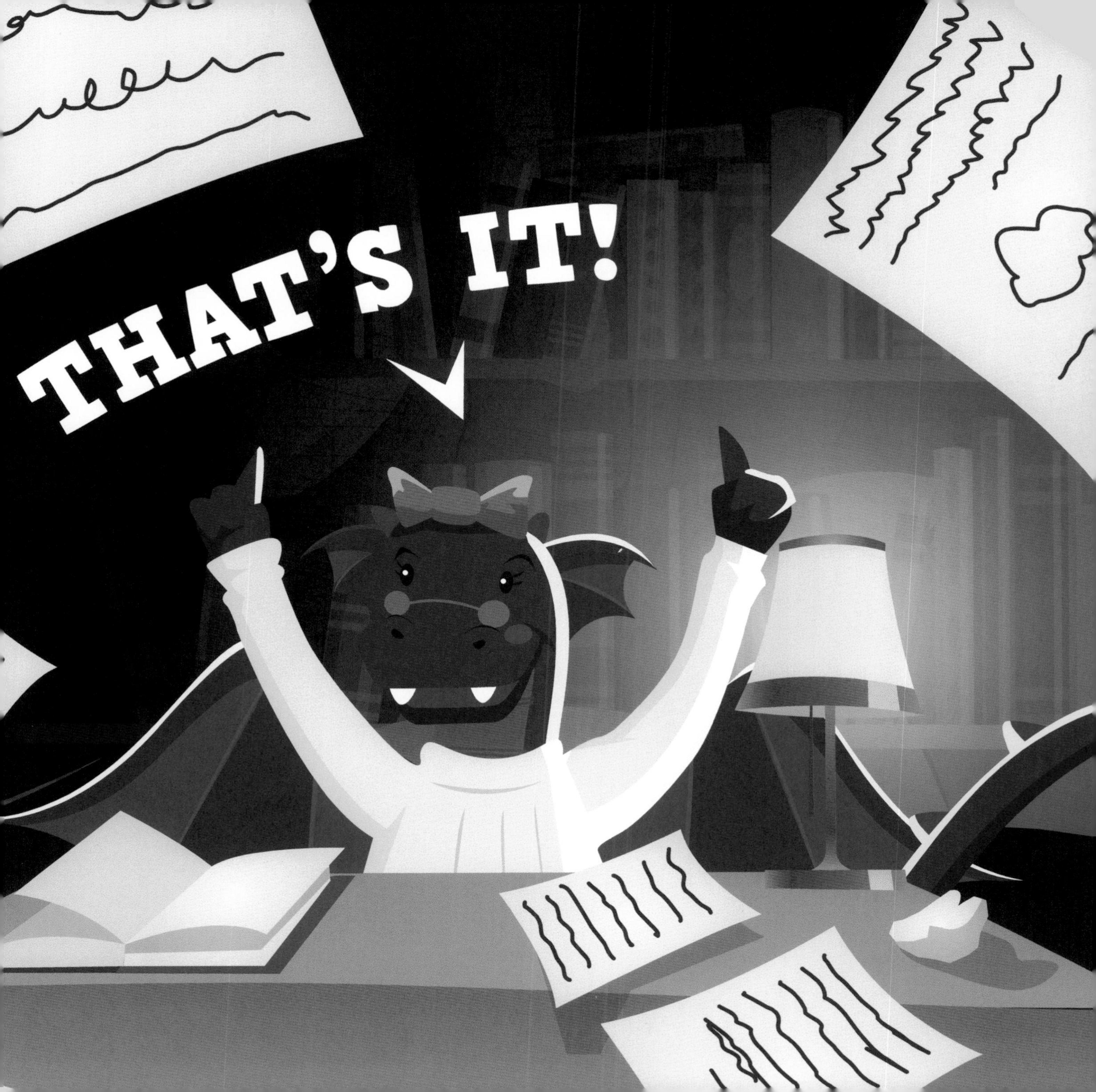
THAT'S IT!

They tinkered on their bikes and polished them so shiny bright,
To have a chance at winning all the details must be right.
The crowds were cheering for the racers ready to take part,
The starting pistol fired and dragons raced off from the start.

Carefully they cornered getting faster on the straight,
Rushing to the finish line, they didn't hesitate.
The dragon in first place then felt a twitching in her nose,
This was a riders nightmare, that or itching on your toes.

AATTTCHOOOO!

She drew in breath to stop the sneeze, alas it was no good,
She sneezed so hard the bike went skidding straight into a wood.
It needed fixing fast before she got back on the track,
She looked around for help and saw ten humans looking back.

There was an awkward silence as they all took in the sight,
No one knew if they should run away or stay and fight.
Nervously a human ran his hand through floppy hair,
And said 'Your bike needs fixing, we can help with the repair'.

The dragon cracked a smile and said 'That's really very kind,
I'd appreciate your help, I've got myself in quite a bind!'
The humans were all friendly and so handy with a spanner,
Mechanically gifted with a very pleasant manner.

She got back in the race and won it with a super time,
Spectators cheered so loudly as she crossed the finish line.
Her team mates wondered how on earth she'd got back in the race,
And why she couldn't keep a sneaky smile from on her face.

They went into the wood, where she had fallen, for a look,
The winning dragon reassured them all was by the book.
She looked down near her feet and saw a spanner on the ground,
She stepped on it and whistled while her race mates looked around.
Finding nothing odd they said 'Amazing! You did well!!'
Millie whispered to the humans 'Thank you, I won't tell!'

The Isle of Dragon humans had a friend who was so helpful,
And in keeping humans secret she had proven fundamental.
This speedy dragon lived nearby and really could be trusted,
She would often help hide human clues so none of them get busted.

Next time you read a book that is a brilliant mystery,
Just think maybe the author is a dragon you can't see.
Look all around, check high and low for clues you may have missed,
For if you find a few you may prove dragons do exist.

Printed in Great Britain
by Amazon